PRIVATE

KEEP OUT

SIMON SPOTLIGHT

An imprint of Simon & Schuster Children's Publishing Division

1230 Avenue of the Americas, New York, New York 10020

Copyright © 2001 Paramount Pictures and Viacom International Inc. All rights reserved.

NICKELODEON, *Jimmy Neutron Boy Genius,* and all related titles, logos, and characters are trademarks of Viacom International Inc.

All rights reserved, including the right of reproduction in whole or in part in any form.

SIMON SPOTLIGHT and colophon are registered trademarks of Simon & Schuster.

Manufactured in the United States of America

First Edition 10 9 8 7 6 5 4 3 2 1

ISBN 0-689-84540-5

Special thanks to Manny Galan
Pencils by Kelsey Shannon

as told to Lara Bergen

illustrated by Jason Fruchter

To my ever faithful robotic
dog, Goddard

—J.N.

my BOOK OF INVENTIONS

by Jimmy Neutron

> Hi, I'm Jimmy Neutron, resident boy genius and inventor extraordinaire of Retroville, U.S.A. I bet you'd like to check out my extremely private and top secret book of inventions, wouldn't you? It's got all my latest projects. The only person who's seen it is my best friend, Carl, but you look like someone who can keep a secret. Well, what are you waiting for?

Simon Spotlight/Nickelodeon

New York   London   Toronto   Sydney   Singapore

This is my greatest invention to date: my ever faithful robotic dog, Goddard. Without Goddard I'd still be locked in a dungeon on a faraway planet. But that's another story. Here are just a few of Goddard's awesome features:

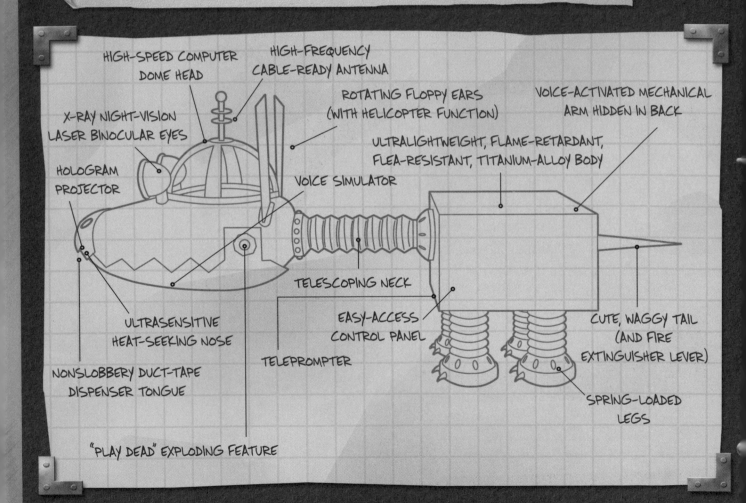

HIGH-SPEED COMPUTER DOME HEAD

HIGH-FREQUENCY CABLE-READY ANTENNA

ROTATING FLOPPY EARS (WITH HELICOPTER FUNCTION)

VOICE-ACTIVATED MECHANICAL ARM HIDDEN IN BACK

X-RAY NIGHT-VISION LASER BINOCULAR EYES

HOLOGRAM PROJECTOR

VOICE SIMULATOR

ULTRALIGHTWEIGHT, FLAME-RETARDANT, FLEA-RESISTANT, TITANIUM-ALLOY BODY

ULTRASENSITIVE HEAT-SEEKING NOSE

TELESCOPING NECK

EASY-ACCESS CONTROL PANEL

TELEPROMPTER

CUTE, WAGGY TAIL (AND FIRE EXTINGUISHER LEVER)

NONSLOBBERY DUCT-TAPE DISPENSER TONGUE

SPRING-LOADED LEGS

"PLAY DEAD" EXPLODING FEATURE

HOLOGRAM PROJECTOR

TELEPROMPTER

HELICOPTER

DIGITAL MOVIE CAMERA

Just about the only thing Goddard can't do is the doggy paddle. He'd rust. But I'm working on that.

Here are some of my favorite pictures of Goddard in action:

Here's me riding Goddard in fly-cycle mode the first time I ever tested it. That was on planet Yolkus.

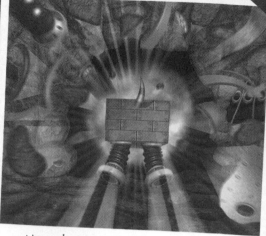

Here's Goddard busting me and my buddies out of a Yokian prison. Good boy, Goddard!

And here's me climbing Goddard in stepladder mode to get to the Yokian control booth.

I originally designed this feature to crack soft-boiled eggs for breakfast. Who knew it would come in so handy on those gooey, slime-filled Yokians?

Here's me using Goddard as binoculars to check out planet Yolkus.

Don't get me wrong. Goddard and I aren't always saving the world as we know it from aliens. Sometimes we just have fun scooting around . . .

. . . and playing ball. (Okay, so maybe a simple game of catch would have been better.)

You can always teach a new dog old tricks. So now you've seen my best invention. But wait! There's more. . . .

From the second I wake up in the morning I've got inventions to help me get ready for school (preferably before I miss the bus). First my solid-fuel rocket alarm clock blasts off. Then I start the gadgets I've programmed to make my bed, get me dressed, tie my shoes, and of course, clean my room.

In my bathroom there are robots to wash my face, brush my teeth, and style my hair (not an easy job).

Then I grab my homework and I'm off to school. Check out my super-useful backpack!

Some days I take the bus to school. But most mornings I take a much more advanced form of transportation.

A flip of the switch and I'm in gravity-bubble mode. Bubble travel is the way of the future.

And if I'm really late I can activate the Neutron backpack full-rocket thrusters. Here's a picture of the thrusters in position.

These are pictures of my classroom and desk at school.

I sit here.

PRESS
APRIL 27

NEUTRON

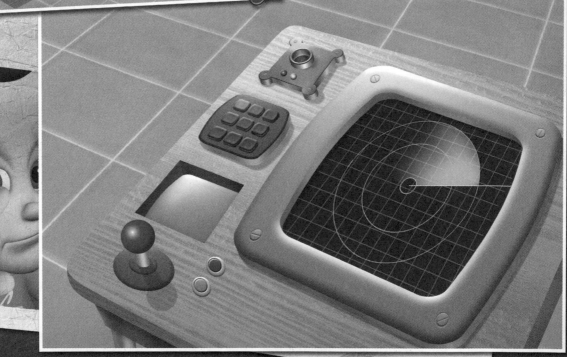

As you can see I've invented several things to help the day go faster. But I've also found that school offers young inventors like me a great chance to test out new devices—show-and-tell.

One time I brought Goddard in for show-and-tell.

Then there was the time I showed my shrink ray to the class. I tried to shrink Cindy Vortex, but it didn't work.

I'm thinking about bringing in a science experiment in progress next week.

After school I hang out with Goddard and my friends Carl and Sheen at my clubhouse.

It's taken awhile, but I think I've finally designed a girl-proof security system.

First my Vox security scanner confirms a DNA match from a strand of my hair.

carl

Sheen

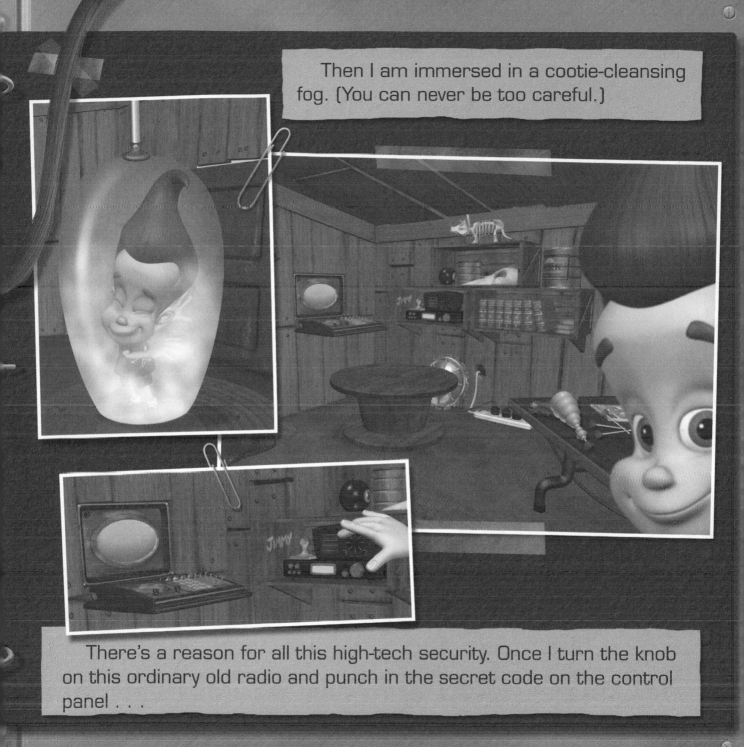

Then I am immersed in a cootie-cleansing fog. (You can never be too careful.)

There's a reason for all this high-tech security. Once I turn the knob on this ordinary old radio and punch in the secret code on the control panel . . .

. . . I arrive at my top secret underground lab. This is where I do most of my inventing, experimenting, and repairing (or *reinventing,* as I like to call it). Let me show you around. . . .

My long-range Space Scanner is mission control whenever I'm saving the world from evil mind-controlling aliens and such.

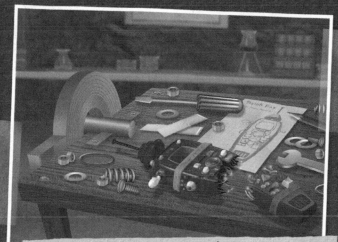

My workbench is complete with duct tape, gum, and other tools. As you can see, I'm still trying to put my shrink ray back together. It's never been the same since that overgrown chicken, Poultra, smashed it.

My Retro-Wrench is my essential tool. Without it I never could have turned a bunch of Retroland rides into intergalactic spaceships.

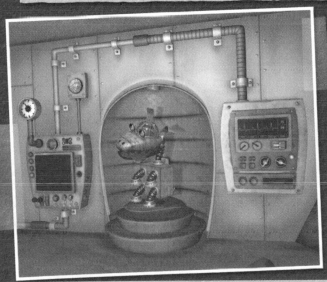

Goddard's bed and recharging station.

My Goddard repair and construction kit.

And then, of course, there are my inventions in progress. . . .

This is Darwin the evolving fish. He's coming along nicely, don't you think?

And watch out for this one. It's a girl-eating plant with an appetite!

And here's one of my favorites: a time accelerator. It came in handy the time I tried to bribe my mom into letting me go to Retroland. I made her a pearl necklace with some oysters and a bunch of sand—in less than twenty minutes! She didn't go for it, though.

I'm still fine-tuning these portable black holes. I hope to use them to travel through time . . .

. . . and help me take out the garbage!

By the time I'm done working on my inventions it's usually dark. And you know what that means. Time for bed . . . NOT! It's time for space travel in my Strato XL Rocket. Look out, universe, here I come!

This is the invention that helped me save Retroville. Well, all of Retroville's grown-ups at least.

TOASTER SATELLITE

ENGINES CAPABLE OF CYCLING AT ONE MILLION GIGAJOULES

RECEPTOR VALVE FOR SILVER FUN FUEL—A COMPLEX COMPOUND MADE FROM PLUTONIUM, LIQUID HYDROGEN, AND A TOUCH OF TAFFY (POWERFUL AND EDIBLE!)

OOPS, LOOKS LIKE I SPILLED A LITTLE FUN FUEL HERE . . . UH, WATCH OUT FOR THAT.

Satellite deployment system (a.k.a. my buddy Carl).

This is Carl testing the ejection seat. He loves that thing.

Here's Goddard handing me my Retro-Wrench as we nosedive toward the Earth's surface. I must have still been working on the thrust-to-fuel ratio at that point. At least we didn't blow up!

And here's me leading the Retroville fleet to planet Yolkus to rescue our parents from aliens. Jumpin' Jupiter!

My trip to planet Yolkus inspired one of my latest and greatest inventions: the parental-unit brainwasher (and dryer). Ta-da!

It's based on an alien mind-control device that I secretly brought back from my Yokian mission. The evil Yokians had used it to keep our parents in a zombielike state until they could feed them to Poultra. What a shocking misuse of science!

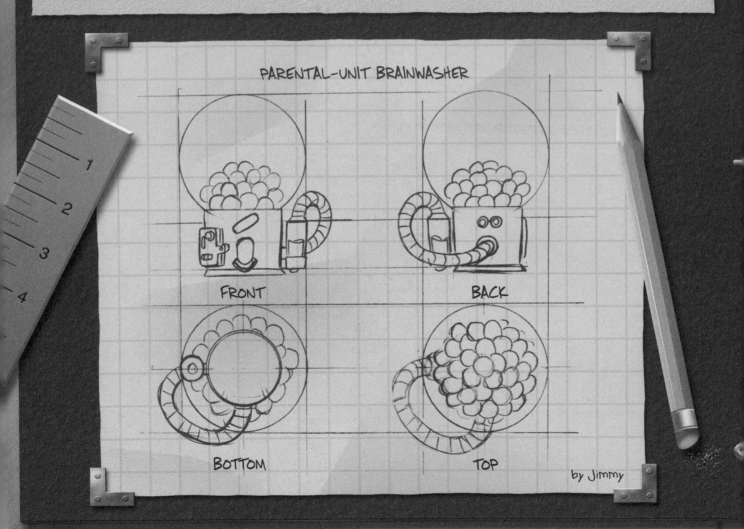

PARENTAL-UNIT BRAINWASHER

FRONT

BACK

BOTTOM

TOP

by Jimmy

Still, no scientific discovery should ever be completely wasted.

I think you'll agree, my inventions could redefine life as we know it and generally make the world a better place. But please keep a lid on it. Who knows what could happen if my top secret book of inventions fell into the wrong hands!